Time for Sch

Written by Wendy Cope

Illustrated by Mike Phillips

Collins

Time for school, so here I come.
Hello teacher. Bye-bye Mum.

Hello friends. Another day –
Hours and hours to work and play.

Books to read and sums to do,

Stories, painting pictures too.

When the bell rings, we go out,

Run around and laugh and shout.

Then back in through the classroom door.

We're quiet again. We work some more.

We sing, we clap, we stamp our feet,

And then, at last, it's time to eat.

More play, more work, all afternoon.
I'm tired. Is it home time soon?

Half past three. Home time has come.
Bye-bye teacher. Hello Mum.

Work and play at school today!

Ideas for reading

Written by Clare Dowdall, PhD
Lecturer and Primary Literacy Consultant

Learning objectives: identify the constituent parts of two-syllable and three-syllable words to support the application of phonic knowledge and skills; identify the main events and characters in stories and find specific information in simple texts; use syntax and context when reading for meaning; visualise and comment on events, characters and ideas, making imaginative links to their own experiences; interpret a text by reading aloud with some variety in pace and emphasis

Curriculum links: Mathematics, Citizenship

High frequency words: school, come, friends, another, day, play, around, through, again, last, three

Interest words: hours, stories, painting, pictures, laugh, classroom, quiet, afternoon, tired

Resources: blank cards, interest-word flashcards, whiteboard

Word count: 100

Getting started

- Ask children to name different times of the day and make a list on the whiteboard, e.g. morning, lunchtime, afternoon, evening, nighttime.

- Look at the cover and read the blurb to the children. Model reading with rhythm and expression. Explain that this story is presented as a poem and needs to be read expressively, paying attention to the rhyme and rhythm. Ask the children to practise reading the blurb with you. Praise them for fluent and expressive reading.

- Introduce the interest words. Look at each word in turn and help children to read it, using phonic knowledge where possible, and applying other strategies where necessary, e.g. looking for chunks that are known already or familiar units of meaning, e.g. *h-our-s, paint-ing*.

Reading and responding

- Turn to pp2–3. Model reading the poem expressively. Ask children to find the words that rhyme. Discuss who is narrating the poem. Check that children understand that the poem is written in the child's voice.

- Ask children to look closely at the pictures on pp2–3 to find out what time of day it is and what the children are doing.

- Ask children to continue reading to the end of the poem in pairs, reading with expression and noticing how the child's day develops.